KT-222-160

P'
T(
or c(
Y(

To my wonderful friend of more than forty years, fellow artist, Allan Markman.

—Douglas Florian

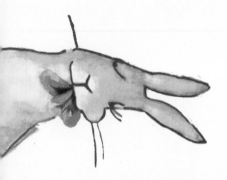

First published in the UK in 2016 by Templar Publishing,
part of the Bonnier Publishing Group,
The Plaza, 535 King's Road, London, SW10 0SZ
www.templarco.co.uk
www.bonnierpublishing.com

First published in the U.S. in 2016 by little bee books,
part of the Bonnier Publishing Group

ISBN 978-1-78370-540-5

Designed by Rob Wall
Edited by Jenna Pocius

Printed in China

The Wonderful Habits of Rabbits

templar publishing

The habits of rabbits are many, not few,

with plenty of things that they love to do!

There's frightening frogs
and discovering moles.

In spring there is smelling
the fragrance of flowers.

In summer there's swimming
and lazing for hours.

In winter there's building
a rabbit of snow.

Of course there is hearing
with great rabbit ears,

and finding lost things
that were buried for years.

There's hitching a ride
on Dad's back, big and strong,

but you have to hold tight
if you want to stay on!

And when you get home,
there's hugging your mother.

There's chewing a carrot
and biting a beet.

And when there is music,
there's thumping your feet.

stretching your arms
and scratching your head.

is saying "goodnight"
with a hug and a kiss.